Click! Flash!

Barbara Applin

MACMILLAN
CARIBBEAN

Macmillan Education
Between Towns Road, Oxford OX4 3PP
A division of Macmillan Publishers Limited
Companies and representatives throughout the world

ISBN 0 333 92077 5

First published 2001

Illustrations by Lynne Willey / JM & A

www.macmillan-caribbean.com

Printed and bound in Malaysia

2008 2007 2006 2005
11 10 9 8 7 6

'It's a camera! The best present ever, Uncle Jimmy!' cried Daniel.

Uncle Jimmy often brought presents when his ship came to the island.

'There's a film in it,' said Uncle Jimmy, 'with twelve shots. And here's another film. After that you have to buy your own. Look through here and then press this. And this is the flash.'

Daniel took a photo of Uncle Jimmy in his uniform. Uncle Jimmy was Purser on a cruise ship. All the passengers liked him. They liked his uniform and they liked his friendly smile.

Daniel took a photo of his sister.
'Keep still, Bella!' he called. 'Don't
wriggle or you'll spoil the photo!'

The next day Daniel took a lot more photos.

His father was carrying plates of food. He was a waiter in the hotel restaurant. He was always in a hurry.

His mother was carrying a pile of towels.
She was a chambermaid. She always had a
friendly smile too.

Daniel took his camera
to the beach. His friends were
playing cricket.

Tomas ran Lenny out
and Daniel got a photo of it.

Jo-Jo took a great catch and
Daniel got a photo of it.

Mandy bowled Jake out and
Daniel got a photo of that too.

Suddenly the camera started to whirr.
Daniel looked at it and read the numbers.
'That's the end of the film,' he said. 'I'll take it
to Mr Samson.'

'The photos will be ready tomorrow,' said Mr Samson. 'That'll be ten dollars.'

Daniel counted his money. 'I'll have to earn some more,' he said.

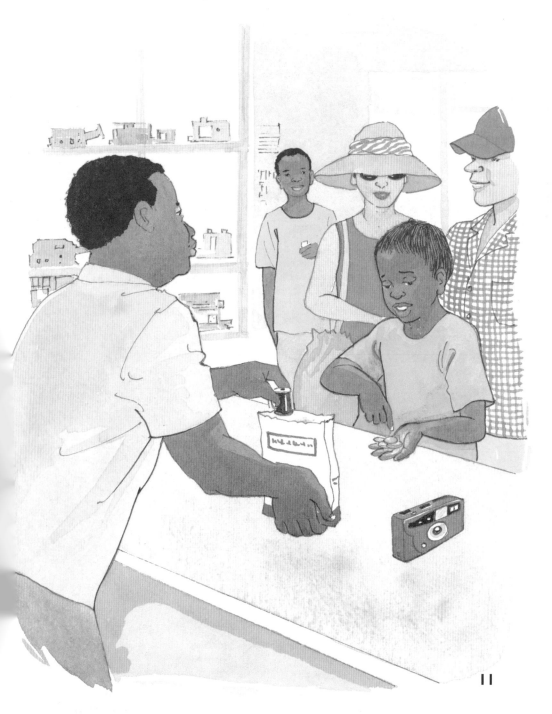

The next morning Daniel went to the golf course. He looked for lost golf balls. There was one in the sand of a bunker. There were six in the tall grass and there was another under the bushes.

The golf pro paid Daniel for the balls.
Now he had enough money. He hurried to
Mr Samson and got his pictures. He bought
another film.

Daniel showed the photos to his friends.
'Oh, dear, that one's too dark,' he said.
But the photo of Bella was lovely.

'Just look at these photos of the cricket
game!' cried Mandy.

'You got your finger in the way on this
one,' said Tomas.

Jo-Jo laughed. 'And your father has no head.'

Daniel took lots of photos on his second film.

'I'll do a close-up of that lizard,' he said. But it got away.

'Now I'll use the flash,' he decided.

He waited until it was dark. Then he crept out of the back door of the hotel and looked around.

There was a creaking noise. Daniel kept still. Someone inside the hotel was opening a window.

'Why doesn't he put on the light?' Daniel wondered.

A leg came over the windowsill, then an arm. The arm was putting something heavy on the ground.

At that moment Daniel pointed his camera. Click! Flash!

Daniel saw a dark shape. It was moving towards him! He hid under the bushes.

Footsteps came near. An arm pushed the bushes back. It came close to his head!
But at last the footsteps went away.

The next morning Daniel took the film to Mr Samson.

Everyone was talking. Daniel heard something about a robbery and a reward, but he didn't really listen. He was thinking about his photos. 'I hope the flash worked!' he thought.

'More photos already!' said Mr Samson.
'Come into my dark room and I'll develop
them now.'

Daniel watched as the pictures came out.

'You're getting better, my boy,' said Mr Samson. 'This photo of the crab is quite good.'

'I wanted a lizard,' said Daniel. 'But it got away.'

Mr Samson held up the last photo. 'My goodness, you've snapped the burglar!' he cried. 'I know him. It's the laundryman at the hotel. Let's take this to the manager. He's offering a reward. That will buy you lots of films!'

CARIBBEAN HOP STEP JUMPS

Series Listing

HOP

Click Flash   Barbara Applin   0-333-92077-5
Ping Pong Pan   Barbara Applin   0-333-74142-0
The School that Sank   Sherry North   0-333-97658-4
Water for Monique Shelley Davidow & Catherine Parrill   0-333-97429-8

STEP

The Angry Mountain   Claudette Megan Adams   0-333-74144-7
Carly and the Crabholes   Natalie Williams   0-333-95445-9
Gary the Smartest Gecko   Thalia Bell   0-333-95446-7
Gyp's Puppies   Sandra Browne   1-4050-2514-X
Ninety-nine Potcakes   Alice Bain   0-333-97659-2
Saving Mr Omardeen   Judy Stone   0-333-77623-2
The Scottish Island Girl   Joanne Johnson   0-333-92091-0
Shauna's Hurricane   Francine Jacobs   1-4050-1701-5

JUMP

Digger's Diner   Joanne Johnson   1-4050-2467-4
Fire and Steel   Judy Stone   0-333-77622-4
Fisherwoman   Effie Adrienne   0-333-74143-9
Go! Krabita! Go!   Petronella Breinburg   0-333-95305-3
Jeremia and the Trumpet Man   Petronella Breinburg   0-333-92065-1
Running for Real   Marcia Francois   0-333-92234-4
Sally's Way   Joanne Johnson   0-333-95450-5
The Taming of Pudding-Pan   Berna McIntosh   0-333-74141-2
The Village Storyteller   Claudette Megan Adams   0-333-97632-0